rudds_childrens_books

This book belongs to...

Everybody loves rainbows,

but do you know what is at the end of a

rainbow?

Many people think there is a big pot

of gold coins, but this is untrue.

In fact at the end of every rainbow there is a
very small door that leads to the magical world

of eggs.

Egg world is filled with the most wonderful and whimsical creatures that you will ever meet.

Some are naughty, some are nice and some are saintly.

Just like the caring and most generous egg of them all...

Father Eggmas.

Now if you don't know who Father Eggmas is, I will tell you a little bit about him.

A long, long time ago when your parents were in nappies, there lived a very generous egg by the name of Saint Nicolas.

Every year Saint Nicolas would dress in his favourite green hat and coat and deliver mince pies under the cover of darkness to all of the poor families' around his village.

Saint Nicolas was also a very brave explorer, so one year for a holiday he decided to visit the North Pole.

The winds blew fierce at the North Pole and the snow began to fall heavier and heavier. In desperation Saint Nicolas fled to a nearby ice cave to shelter from the horrific storm.

This cave that he had stumbled on was no ordinary cave, it was in fact the home of some very magical and tiny creatures called Elves.

The Elves could see the kindness in his heart and decided that they would help him deliver toys instead of mince pies to all of the poor families' around the world.

Saint Nicolas thought that this was an impossible task, as he could not possibly travel around the world in such a small amount of time.

The Elves giggled and told him of a magical creature called a reindeer, who could fly faster than lightning.

You see the reindeers' lived next to the magnetic field of the North Pole and in turn had evolved to repel the magnetic forces, which made the reindeers' fly at tremendous speeds.

Saint Nicolas searched high and low for these magical creatures and eventually found eight babies that had been abandoned.

He raised the baby reindeers' and soon became their Father.

Because of this he decided to change his name to Father Eggmas. He also decided that same day to change his green hat and coat to match the colours of the stripy North Pole, which were bright red and gleaming white.

All was going well until one Elf named Gumble informed Father Eggmas that as well as delivering all of the gifts, that he should reward every child that shows the same saintly qualities as he does.

So Father Eggmas and all of the Elves put their head's together and came up with a naughty and nice list, this would separate the good eggs from the bad eggs.

One year Father Eggmas forgot to deliver a toy to a very good child called Shelly.

Father Eggmas quickly realised his mistake and gave Shelly extra gifts that year to say sorry for his mistake.

From that day forward he vowed always to check his naughty and nice list twice.

As the years past on, so grew the legend of Father Eggmas and soon every child that had been good all year round, found the most wonderful and whimsical toys under their tree.

All the naughty children that had been bad all year round, did not find wonderful toys, instead they found lumps of dirty, black coal.

As more and more children were being extremely good, Father Eggmas ended up delivering more and more gifts, this meant that sometimes he would forget to eat his breakfast, lunch and dinner.

So out of appreciation, it became customary to leave out some nice warm mince pies, gingerbreads and some carrots for the reindeers'.

Father Eggmas loved this gesture, although sometimes he only had time to nibble them.

So now you know more about Father Eggmas and his origin story.

There is something that Father Eggmas wants to know about you in return.

Have you been a naughty egg this year or a nice one?

I guess you will find out on Eggmas Eve.

Merry Christmas

The End.

Printed in Great Britain
by Amazon